P9-BII-742

Everything You Need To Know

WHEN A PARENT DIES

Children in a family must take on new responsibilities when a parent dies.

• THE NEED TO KNOW LIBRARY •

Everything You Need To Know

WHEN A PARENT DIES

Fred Bratman

THE ROSEN PUBLISHING GROUP, INC.
NEW YORK

For Jack's Memory

Published in 1992 by The Rosen Publishing Group, Inc.
29 East 21st Street, New York, NY 10010

First Edition

Printed in Canada

Library of Congress Cataloging-in-Publication Data

Bratman, Fred.
Everything you need to know when a parent dies/
Fred Bratman. — 1st ed.
(The Need to know library)
Includes bibliographical references and index.
Summary: A guide to coping with the stresses and emotions arising after the death of a parent.
ISBN 0-8239-1324-4
1. Bereavement in children—Juvenile literature. 2. Parents–death—Psychological aspects—Juvenile literature. 3. Children and death—Juvenile literature. 4. Grief in children—Juvenile literature. [1. Death. 2. Parent and child.] I. Title. II. Series.
BF723.G75873 1991
155.9'37—dc20 90-27488
CIP
AC

Contents

Introduction

Death is not an easy thing to think about. It's not an easy thing to talk about. Even grown-ups have a difficult time talking about it. That's because talking about death makes people understand that one day they will die.

This book is about a very difficult thing to think about—the death of a parent. It will help you learn to deal with the loss of a parent. It will help you understand the scary feelings that come after a parent dies. It will help you see the many different ways people feel when someone close to them dies. The feeling we have when someone we love dies is called *grief*.

The death of a parent is different from the loss of anyone else. There is a special link between you and your parents. You may have lost a grandparent, uncle, sister, or even a pet who was very special to you. But a parent has a one-of-a-kind bond with you. A parent's death will shake you more powerfully than any other. It can feel like a hard kick in the stomach.

The death of a parent can greatly change your life. It can mean a big change in the way a family lives. It may mean finding a job to help the family meet its expenses. Or helping out at home a lot more. If your parents are divorced, you may have to move to another city to be with your living parent. You may have to move in with a relative. You may have to live in a foster home. But this book will also explain how your rights are protected. Whatever happens, you will be well taken care of.

In this book you will read stories about other children whose parents died. You will learn what they did to ease their pain.

Many of you have healthy parents who aren't going to die for years. But perhaps a friend of yours will lose a parent. This book will tell you how you can help your friend. It will tell you things to say and do. A true friend shares good and bad times. You will also learn where to get help from grown-ups who are trained to work with people who are sad.

The death of a parent is a very painful and difficult loss. The feelings and fears we have after we lose someone special are what makes us human. But remember that you are not alone. There are ways to cope with what has happened. The painful feelings you have are nothing to be ashamed of. They make you aware of the importance of your loss. You need to talk about your feelings. If you do not face them, they will not go away. If you learn to live with your feelings, you will become stronger. But it takes a lot of time.

The death of a parent can make it hard for children to concentrate or think of anything else.

Chapter 1

The Nightmare Is True

Janet's Diary

It doesn't make sense. I feel numb. My father is dead. I still can't believe it. I refuse to believe it. This must be a nightmare. I thought old or sick people died. My father wasn't old. My father didn't look sick. But he's dead. It's the most unfair thing in the world. My life will never be the same again.

Janet is right. The death of a parent is a nightmare. It is unfair and cruel. It doesn't matter whether your parent has been sick for months or whether he or she died suddenly, without any warning. Your reaction is likely to be the same. Like Janet, at first you'll be shocked. You won't believe that your parent is really dead. Because it's so painful, you'll try to deny that it has happened. The sad fact is that no matter how much you deny it, your parent is dead. Nothing can change that fact.

Death makes you aware of your limits. All living things die. You may have already had a pet cat, dog, or bird that died. Or perhaps a grandparent. For most people, the death of a parent is the most painful loss that can be suffered.

That's because you are usually closer to your parents than to anyone else. The close link between parent and child exists for nearly all animals. Go to a zoo and watch how a lioness cares for her cubs. She feeds, cleans, and protects them. They would die without her care. That's why the death of a parent hurts so much.

People don't always live to an old age. Illness, accidents, suicide, and murder happen to people of all ages. Even so, the average person does live to be about 75 years old. Most people expect to live a long, full life.

Denying Death

Janet's father wasn't given a choice. He died suddenly, without any warning. Many kids react to their parent's death like Janet did. At first they are shocked. They can't accept what has happened. They try to push the idea out of their heads. Psychologists are trained to understand feelings. They call this kind of feeling *denial.*

Denial is a natural reaction to almost any bad event. Even grown-ups use denial as a reaction to horrible events. At first, you may try to deny to yourself that your parent is dead. You hope that your mother or father will come back to life. As the weeks and months pass, you will slowly come to accept your loss.

Nearly everyone whose parent dies feels cheated. That is easy to understand. People who love their parents want to have them around. The death of a parent is one of the most painful examples of life's unfairness. You may ask yourself, "Why me?" You may feel that your life will never be the same. You may be afraid that from now on only horrible things will happen to you. This isn't true.

Death is not easy to understand. Thinking about it makes many people sad or depressed. When you are a teenager, death is even harder to understand. Your body is growing and changing. Adulthood is just around the corner. Life is on your mind, not death. The natural reaction is to try and shut it out. Many kids who lose a parent fear that they will die too. But most young people are strong and healthy. They have full lives ahead of them.

Life Can Change

The death of a parent may lead you to ask a lot of hard questions. These questions don't have quick or easy answers. They are the kind of questions people have asked for thousands of years.

Don't expect to be able to understand death, at least not right away.

The death of a parent can seriously change a child's life. The weeks and months following a death are very hard. For some kids it may mean moving to a different apartment or house. You may even have to move to a different part of the country. This kind of a move is never easy. You may have to say goodbye to old friends and make new ones. A new place can be scary. Don't expect to feel at home right away. Give yourself a break. This is not the time to put pressure on yourself.

Janet's mother sent her to live with her grandparents. They lived in another city, hundreds of miles away. Janet was angry with her mother's decision. The move meant Janet would have to go to a different school. But her mother didn't feel she could give Janet the care and attention she deserved. She had a lot of things to work out. And she was very sad, too.

If you don't want to move, talk to your parent. Often the move is just for a short time. Your parent may need time to settle family problems. You may be able to move back home after a few weeks.

Some kids are sent to live with foster parents. A foster parent offers to provide a home and care to children who are not relatives. A social service agency matches the child with the right foster parents. This makes it easier for the children to feel at home sooner. Foster care is not a sign that your living parent doesn't want you. It can give your

Things can change dramatically when a family loses a parent. Sometimes it is necessary for the remaining family to sell their house or move to another neighborhood.

living parent time to find a job, or a different place for the family to live. For many kids, foster care is only temporary. They are sent back home within a few weeks.

You may not be sent to live with a relative or foster parents. But there could still be major changes in your life. The death of a parent is more than the loss of love and support. It often means the loss of a salary to the family. With that loss of income, a family's lifestyle can change. These changes are never easy.

After Steve's father died, his family had to move to a smaller apartment in another part of town. Steve's mother had to get a full-time job even to afford the new, smaller apartment.

For Steve's family, there was less money to go around. This could happen to your family if a parent dies. His mother worked part-time before his father died. But Steve's family needed his father's salary. Now the family would have to change the way they lived. Steve's mom spent less money for food. They didn't have meat for dinner all the time. There was less money for clothes and fun activities.

Steve got an after-school job to help his family. Many kids who lose a parent get a part-time job to help out. The money can help keep the family together. Helping out can make a young person feel important to the family. This sometimes helps ease the pain of *grieving* (feeling sad) for the lost parent.

Chapter 2

A Flood of Feelings

Ricky's Diary

I was sitting in my room when my uncle walked in. He came over and sat down next to me. I was looking at some photos we took last summer on vacation. He told me how I was the man in the house now that my father was dead. He said I wasn't a kid any longer and that I would have to do more. He said my mom would rely on me more to help. That my brothers and sisters need me to be their father. I want to help. But I don't know how much I can do.

Kids have a very hard time when a parent dies. They are often expected to act like grown-ups. But they are usually treated like kids. What's worse, they are asked to become adults overnight. Becoming an adult is a slow, gradual process. It takes years. But often when a parent dies, your living parent or a close relative may tell you that you have to grow up. But you may not feel ready to be an adult.

Ricky's uncle probably thought he was doing the right thing. He believed it was time to treat Ricky like an adult. But Ricky is a kid. He can't become an adult just because his uncle tells him he should. It's hard to skip over stages of growing up.

Ricky has a lot of anger. He doesn't want to believe that his dad is gone. Ricky is very sad at night. He spent time with his father after he finished his homework every night. Ricky is so angry that he feels like screaming.

At school Ricky's mind wanders. "My father's death is the most unfair thing in the world," he thinks. He doesn't listen in class. His teachers try to be understanding. And things have gotten worse since he started to skip school.

The principal called Ricky's mother. She told his mother that Ricky's grades were slipping. She also told her that Ricky had been cutting school. The principal said she understood that Ricky's father had died. But Ricky had to straighten up, she said. He was running out of chances. When Ricky got home, his mother was in the living room crying. He had seen her crying a lot lately. But this time, Ricky knew he was in trouble.

Friends are an important source of comfort and security during times of great sadness.

Even though a parent is gone, his or her memory will stay with you for the rest of your life.

"I expected you to act like an adult. But you are acting like a child," she told him. "I have a lot on my mind. I don't need to get a call from school to hear the principal complain about you. You are the oldest. I expect you to be a help. I expect you to help with your brothers and sisters. I'm disappointed in you."

Ricky was sorry that he had upset his mother. But he was also angry. Too much was being asked of him and it was too soon.

It is natural to feel a flood of emotions when your parent dies. You may be shocked, angry, or numb. You probably feel helpless and frightened. The only way to go on is to make believe your parent didn't die. Of course, you know that's not true. But you act as though your parent were still alive. This is called a *defense.* A defense is a way of holding off and denying the flood of emotions you feel.

Ricky has to tell his mother how scared and angry he feels. He has to tell her that he cannot act like an adult right away. He should also tell her how much he misses his father. This is the first and most important step on the way to accepting the death.

Ricky may not feel that he can talk to his mother about these things. But he can have a talk with his pastor, priest or rabbi. He can talk to the school guidance counselor. (At the back of the book, you'll find other places to get help).

Caring for a parent who is terminally ill takes great courage and compassion.

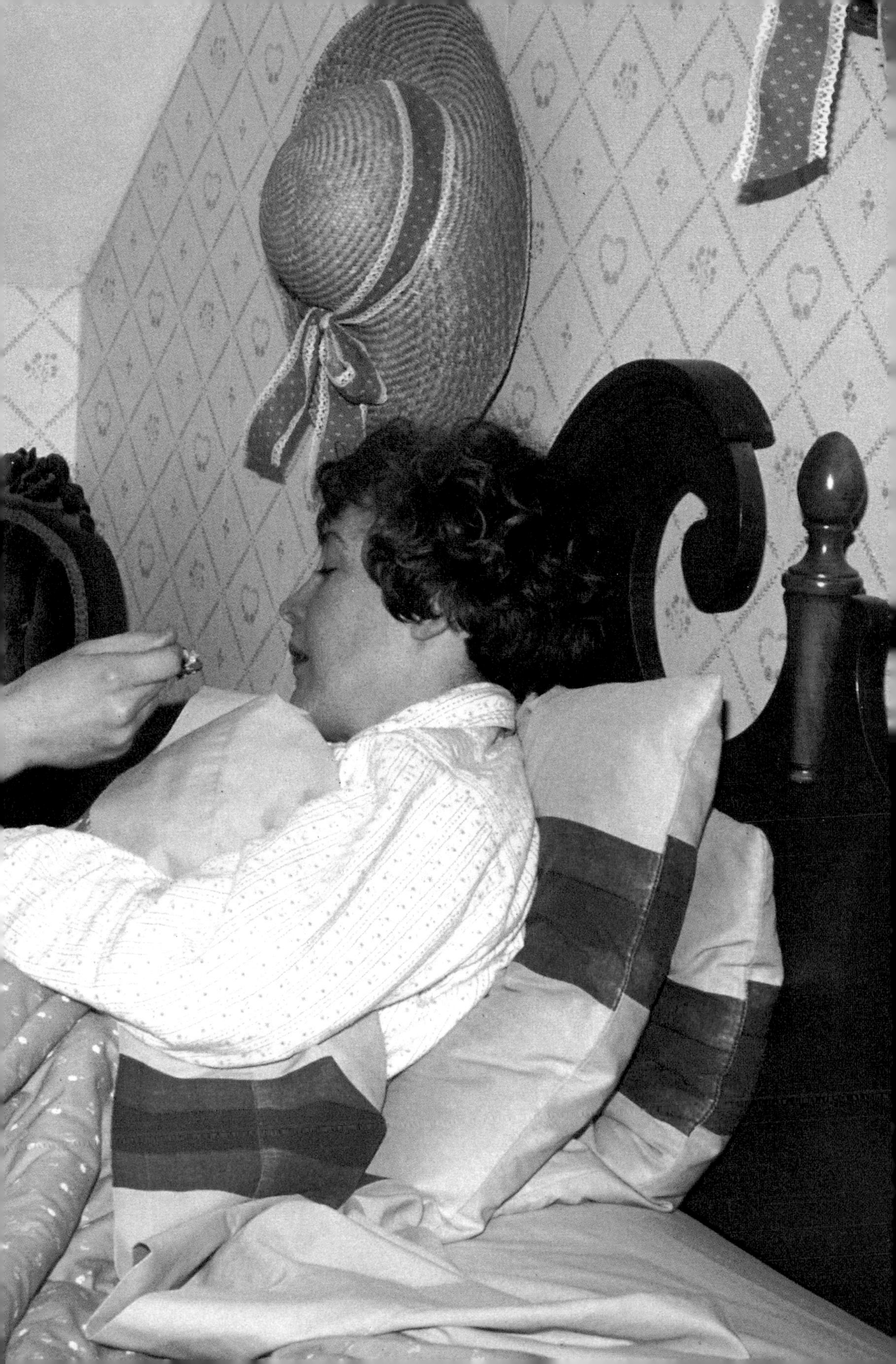

It's Not Your Fault

Beatrice's mother died shortly after the two of them had a big fight. They usually got along well, but once in awhile they'd argue. Her mother wanted Beatrice to stop seeing William. They yelled and screamed at each other. Her mother said Beatrice was too young to spend all her time with one boy. She also said Beatrice wasn't spending enough time studying. Her grades were slipping. Less than a week later, Beatrice's mother died of a heart attack. Beatrice may have been angry with her mother, but she loved her. She didn't want her mother to die.

Beatrice blamed herself for her mother's death. She told her friend Martha that her mother died because of the fight. She said she got her mother so upset that she died. Beatrice said that if she hadn't fought with her mother, she'd still be alive. She couldn't stop crying.

Martha tried to calm Beatrice. She said that the fight and her mother's death were not related. She reminded Beatrice that her mother had been sick for many years.

"Your mother's doctor told her to give up smoking and to exercise," Martha said. "But she kept on doing things that were bad for her." Beatrice knew that Martha was right. But she still felt guilty.

Fights between kids and parents are a normal part of growing up. Conflict is a part of life. It

The family order often changes after the death of a parent. In many cases, older siblings must assume the role of caretaker for younger family members.

happens between husband and wife, teacher and student, and parent and child. People often see things differently, and they often disagree.

Beatrice blamed herself for something she had no control over. She knew that her mother had been sick. She knew her mother hadn't been taking good care of herself. The fight Beatrice had with her mother had upset her mother. But her mother had not been well for a long time.

Some kids treat themselves differently when a parent dies. Then they do things that could hurt them. They eat too much. Or they drink alcohol or take drugs. They do these things to get away from their feelings of sadness. But these things don't help. Feelings of sadness will return again and again. You cannot escape your feelings. You have to face them.

Some kids are so angry after a parent dies that they lash out. They get into fights or damage property. It is a way to let out their anger. But these actions don't help. And the kids can get into trouble at school. They can even get into trouble with the police.

Something really terrible happens to some kids. They get so sad that they think of suicide (killing themselves). They say that they don't want to live anymore. They want to be with their dead parent. All kids feel sadness, anger, and deep loss when a parent dies. But these feelings don't last forever. As time passes, life returns to normal.

Chapter 3

Grieving from a Distance

These days, living with one parent is very common. Many, many kids live with either their mom or dad. Some kids live with their grandparents or other relatives. That doesn't have to change the love you feel for the parent who doesn't live with you.

Anne's parents were divorced. Her father now lived in another part of town. She saw her father on weekends and lived with him during the summer school break. Her father had remarried. He had a son and a daughter with his new wife. Anne enjoyed her visits with her father. But she didn't like her father's new wife. Anne said her father's wife was mean to her.

One day Anne got home from her after-school job at the supermarket as the phone rang. Her father's wife was very upset. Anne's father had been shot. "The funeral is Wednesday at 9 a.m. Have your mother drive you over to the church by 8:30."

Anne started to cry. She couldn't believe what she had heard. She felt like she'd been given an electric shock. Her mother asked, "What's wrong?"

"Dad is dead. He was killed in a robbery." "I won't miss your father," her mother said. "He left me in the middle of the night without a dime." Anne stood there crying.

Anne's mother was not thinking about Anne's feelings. She was only thinking about the pain Anne's father had caused her. What Anne needed was support from her mother. She needed someone to share her grief with. She needed someone who would make her feel safe. Her mother was not able to give this to Anne. She was still angry at Anne's father, even though they were divorced 10 years ago.

For Anne, her father was still her father. She still loved him. Anne's mother doesn't understand Anne's feelings. This happens often in families where parents are divorced. Anne's father was kind to her. He didn't stop being her father when he moved out. Things were different for her mother. He did stop being her husband.

At the funeral, her father's wife spoke only a few words to Anne. There were many people there who she had never seen before. She felt like an outsider.

It can be difficult to grieve the loss of a parent in a family where the divorce or separation has already caused anger and pain.

Anne sat next to an uncle who had always been warm to her. They talked about how sad they were about her father's death. They told stories about the good times they had together. Anne felt less alone. She felt comfortable crying in front of her uncle. A few days later her uncle called to see how she was doing. They spoke for nearly an hour. They laughed and cried and remembered more stories about her father.

When You Are Far Away

Anne was lucky. She saw her father often after her parents divorced. That isn't always possible. Sometimes a parent leaves home and moves to a new city hundreds of miles away. This is hard on kids. They don't get to see that parent often. Sometimes they get together only once or twice a year. They only see each other at holidays, or during the summer. Sometimes they cannot visit at all.

Even a child who didn't see his parent often feels angry and sad when that parent dies. He or she probably thought that someday they would spend time together. The child is angry because that dream is taken away.

What happens to kids whose parents are divorced when the parent they are living with dies? Their living parent may live hundreds of miles away in another state. He or she may have a new family.

There is no single answer.

Counselors can help people sort out feelings of grief, confusion, and loneliness.

Some parents eagerly want their children to live with them and their new families. But many times this is not possible.

In some cases, a state or local child care agency will get involved. You will be interviewed by a case worker. You may appear in front of judge in family court. You are not there because you have done anything wrong. It's the judge's job to make sure that your new home is the best one for you.

Sometimes the best place to send you is to your grandparents or other close relatives. When this is not possible, you may be placed with foster parents.

Daniel's mother moved more than 2,000 miles away when she divorced. Daniel spoke to his

Ordinary things around the house will remind the family of the parent it has lost.

mother on the telephone. But sometimes weeks would pass between calls. Daniel wouldn't have much to say to his mom. Daniel used to spend two weeks with his mother each summer. But he skipped his visit this year. He didn't feel comfortable around his mother anymore. The last time they got together they argued a lot. Daniel wasn't sure what he wanted to do after he finished high school.

One night when Daniel was sitting around watching television, the phone rang. It was one of his mother's friends. He told Daniel that he had bad news for him. His mother was dead.

Living apart from a parent doesn't make death less painful for kids. Even though Daniel was not getting along with his mother, he could still remember the good times they had together. The importance of a relationship is not based on whether your parent lives with you. There is more to it than that. The way you feel about the person is what's important. If what you remember is good, then you will probably be very sad.

When a child loses a parent who lives far away, he or she grieves just like other kids. Except it's harder. Your friends may not understand why you are so upset. Perhaps they never met your mom or dad. They don't know how strong your feelings are. Your grief is as painful as it would be if the parent lived with you. You have a right to feel sadness, no matter how far away your parent lived.

Visiting a hospital can be a scary and uncomfortable experience. It requires courage to fulfill the responsibility you may have to a loved one.

Chapter 4

In the Hospital

Jason knew his mother was sick. But he didn't know she was seriously ill. She had been sick for nearly six months. She had been seeing several different doctors. At dinner one night his mom told Jason that she had to go to the hospital. She needed an operation. Jason was scared.

"I'm not going to treat you like a baby," she told him. "I'll tell you what I know. The doctors tell me that I have cancer." Jason couldn't believe his ears. His mother looked healthy to him. "I'll be in the hospital at least a week, maybe longer," she said. "I'll need you to help out with your sister while I'm away from home."

Jason didn't know what to say. He opened his mouth but no words came out. The next day Jason's mother went to the hospital. After school, Jason went to visit her. She was sitting up in bed, but she looked weak. A tube was connected to her arm. She had trouble speaking.

Jason felt like he was in a bad dream. "If only I could wake up," he thought. Then the sadness would go away. But this wasn't a dream.

The nurses and doctors came into the room. Jason asked a doctor what was wrong with his mother. The doctor told Jason that his mother was sick. He said he was going to do all he could to make her well again.

"There's so much I want to say," Jason said to a friend. "But I don't know where to start, I don't want to say anything stupid."

Jason didn't know what to say to his mother. He had only known her as a strong woman. He didn't understand how she could have become weak so quickly.

If your parent is sick in a hospital, figuring out what to say is often hard. You may even feel that the person in the bed is different from your parent. Remember that he or she is the same person. The only difference is that he or she is sick.

Try to talk the way you would if your parent wasn't in a hospital. If you usually talked about your school work, bring in some school work to show your mom or dad. If you both always like to

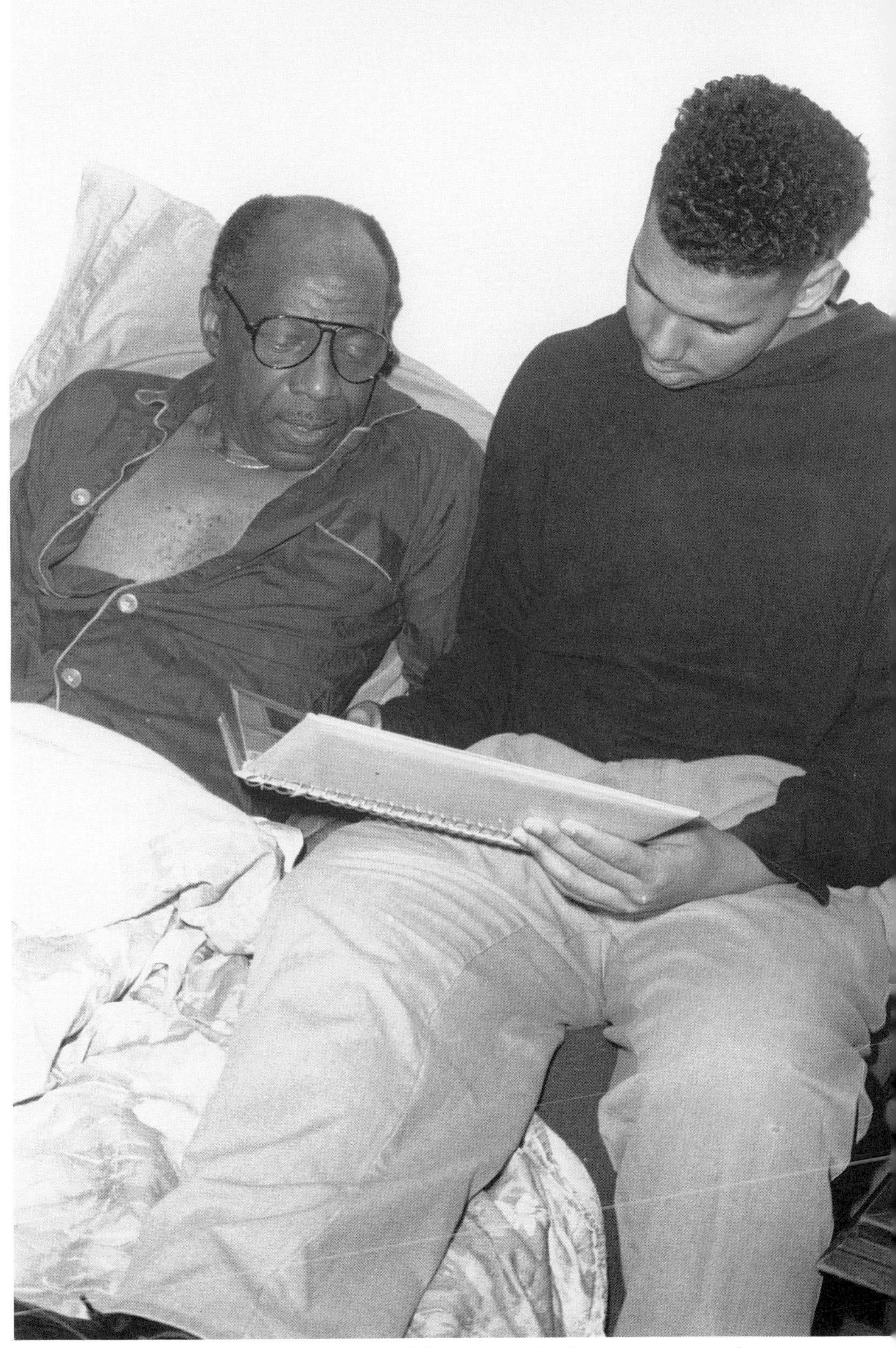

The most comforting thing for a sick person is the company of others.

talk about sports, talk about the latest games and team standings.

Sometimes other adults will tell you what to say in the hospital. They'll say, "Smile, don't let her see you upset. Don't upset her." These adults mean well. But faking it could easily make matters worse. Be honest. Tell your parent how you feel. Parents want to know that they still matter to you. Tell your parent that you really need him or her. But try not to make your parent worry about you. Try to be bright and cheerful.

When your parent is in the hospital, he or she will worry about how life is at home. Your parent will want to know who is cooking for you. He or she will ask about who's helping you with your algebra homework. If you are the oldest child at home, much of the work will fall to you. You may resent the added chores. You may think that school work is enough to keep you busy. But illness in a family means that everyone has to help.

Jason's mother asked him to pick up his younger sister after school every day and bring her to a neighbor. He was also responsible now for buying groceries. And he had to do the laundry for the family. The added work meant that he had to quit the track team. This made Jason angry. He thought he had a chance to make the state championships. He wanted to be helpful at home. But he also wanted to do some things for himself.

All the added work had a bad effect on Jason. He easily became angry at his younger sister. She was giving him a lot of trouble. Jason had to understand something important. His sister was also scared by what was happening to their mother.

At school, Jason's grades were slipping. Grades often drop when a student's parent is very ill. Jason told his teacher that his mother was in the hospital. He explained that he had to help around the house. "I didn't have time to do my homework," Jason said. The teacher said that the work had to be done. But she said that Jason could turn it in to her after his mother got home from the hospital.

Jason's mother returned home after the operation. But over the next year she often had to go for treatment of her cancer. She became weaker. Jason had to continue to do more work at home. He was often tired. He was angry at his mother's illness. Many kids like Jason feel this way. You may feel cheated. You may also feel that life is unfair. These feelings are completely normal. Don't make things worse by getting angry at yourself for feeling this way. Accept your feelings. Let people close to you know how you feel. Talking about your feelings can make you feel better.

A few months later, Jason's mother had to go back to the hospital. The cancer had come back. Jason visited her after school. He could see she was getting weaker. It was harder for her to speak.

Writing down your thoughts and emotions in a diary can often help you cope with troubling times.

Jason's aunt came to live with him and his sister. That made things at home easier.

Jason tried to cheer up his mother when he visited. But she no longer had the energy even to keep her eyes open. Jason knew she was dying. He continued to visit her. But seeing his mother so sick made Jason very upset.

Jason wanted to visit his mother. But there are many boys and girls who don't feel that way. They say that visiting their sick parents is very upsetting. These kids love their parents just as much as Jason loves his mother. But they find it very hard to visit in hospitals. There are times when a person must put aside personal feelings so they can do something more important. Sometimes it is important to grant a dying person's wish or to do things you know will make a sick person happy. Most of the time it is enough to be there and to show support. Finding the strength to put your discomfort aside is not easy. But making sacrifices for those who mean a lot to you is one responsibility of growing up.

Cancer and some other diseases can be *terminal.* This means that they cause death. When a parent has an illness that can't be cured, he or she may stay in the hospital, go home, or go to live their last days in a *hospice.* A hospice is a place for people with terminal illnesses. If your parent needs medical attention, he or she must stay in the hospital. You may want your sick parent to come home. But this is not always possible.

A terminally ill parent may be able to come home to stay with the family. Even though your parent is dying, being home can make him or her feel better. Being in familiar surroundings, close to the people he or she loves, is comforting. But you will probably have more to do around the house. You may find it difficult to act like you did before your parent got sick. This happens to many kids. Don't worry. What your parent needs most now is to be in a safe, familiar setting and to be near you, no matter how you act.

As you have already read, some people who are dying go to live at a hospice. You are allowed to visit your parent in a hospice. Doctors, nurses and counselors at a hospice are trained to work with patients who are dying. They try to make the dying person as comfortable as possible. They also work with the families. They are trained to help people deal with their feelings of grief and sadness.

No one knows, including the doctors, when a patient is going to die. Not knowing can be painful and confusing. There will be good days, when your sick parent seems to be recovering. In terminal cases the good days will not last. But your company can make the good days even better. You will be able to enjoy them with your parent.

Spending time with a terminally ill parent is difficult and scary. But when you look back on that time you will have many good memories.

Strains on the family budget may make it necessary for children to make extra money at part-time jobs.

Funerals are important rituals that allow mourners a chance to grieve and an opportunity to say a final good-bye.

Chapter 5

The Funeral

After your parent dies, there will probably be a funeral. A funeral serves an important purpose. It gives the family a chance to share grief with relatives and friends. Funerals are painful experiences. At a funeral you must face the fact that your parent has died. But funerals can also be comforting. A funeral is a chance to say goodbye to your parent. Your friends and family are there with you to ease your pain.

Funerals are usually led by a pastor, priest, or rabbi. He or she will probably say prayers. The priest will talk about your parent's life and the sadness of his or her death. You may feel that what is being said leaves out too many good things. Remember that the pastor, priest, or rabbi didn't know your lost parent as well as you did.

Often, friends and relatives are also given a chance to speak. They tell stories that show how much your parent was liked and respected. Someone may even tell a joke that shows your parent's sense of humor. The funeral gives people a chance to express what your parent's life and friendship meant to them.

Your living parent may decide that you shouldn't attend the funeral. She or he may think you are too young. Or he or she may think that the experience will be too painful for you. But talk it over with your parent. Explain that you understand the purpose of a funeral. Explain that you wish to say goodbye to your parent with the rest of the family and friends. Say that you will feel left out and upset if you cannot go. After you've calmly told your parent about your feelings, plan to attend.

You may decide that you don't want to attend the funeral. If you don't feel you can handle it, say no. Don't push yourself. Boys often get a hard time from the family if they say they don't want to attend. You have to make people understand how you feel.

Brian's uncle tried to bully Brian. He wanted Brian to go to his mother's funeral. "Act like a man," his uncle said. But Brian was too upset over her death. He didn't think he could handle being with so many people. He told his uncle that he loved his mother very much. But he didn't want to go.

Attending the funeral isn't a sign of how much you loved your parent. You may want to say goodbye in your own way. You may want to grieve in private. Hopefully, your family will understand if you don't want to go to the funeral.

What Happens At A Funeral

Sometimes the funeral is held in a church. Other funerals are held at places called *funeral homes.* The funeral home director and the staff will help your family with the arrangements. Some funerals are small and quiet. Some funerals are attended by a lot of people, and there are many speakers. At a church funeral, sometimes there is music by a choir, or an organist.

The wooden box that holds the body is called the *coffin.* At the funeral, the coffin may be open or closed. Some people want the coffin open. They say it is a last chance to see the dead person. Others want the coffin closed. They say they want to remember the person as he or she looked when he or she was alive.

If the coffin is open, you will have to decide whether you want to see the body. Some grown-ups may try to discourage you. Others may encourage you. There is no right decision. Whether you see the body or not won't change how much you loved your parent when he or she was alive. This isn't a test of bravery. Before you decide, think about how you will feel about seeing the body.

You may decide that you wish to speak at the funeral. This is a decision you should reach with your living parent. If he or she agrees, then you will have a chance to say a few words. You can express how much your parent meant to you. This speech is called a *eulogy.* You should write down what you want to say. You might have a short story to tell that shows your parent's understanding and love.

But don't feel that you must speak at the funeral. You may be too sad to say anything. Your family and friends understand that this is a painful and difficult time for you.

You may be surprised at the funeral by the sad reaction of other family members and friends. You may have never seen your father cry, or your mother break down. Crying is not a sign of weakness. It is a sign of grieving. Their behavior may make you uncomfortable or scared. But they are just expressing their grief. That is what a funeral is for. Don't feel that you must help your grieving parent. What you should do is deal with your own grief.

After the service at the funeral home, the body is usually taken to the cemetery for burial. Going to a cemetery is very hard. It can even be scary. But seeing the coffin put into the ground is another way to see how final the death is. And that memory will help you cope with your loss better in the time to come. Some people are placed in *mausoleums.* These are buildings where caskets are stored above ground. Spaces are cut in the walls for the coffins. These places are called vaults.

Close family and friends are an important source of support during periods of crisis.

Some people tell their families to have their body burned, or *cremated.* The remaining ashes are given to the family. Some people put the ashes in a vase called an *urn,* and keep the ashes at home. Sometimes the ashes are spread over a place that had special meaning to the dead person. Larry's father loved to fish. His ashes were scattered over his favorite lake.

Some people don't want to be buried. They write wills asking their family to give their body to medicine. Their body's organs are then used in transplants. A cornea transplant can give sight to a blind person. Some organs can be taken from a dead person to save the life of another who is sick or dying. People who donate their body to medicine say they do it because they want their last act of life to help others. But some religions forbid transplants.

There are many different ideas about what happens to people after they die. Some believe that each person has a soul that even death can't destroy. Others believe that dead people continues to live through their children. The children's lives are reflections of the lost parent. Many people feel that a dead person remains "alive" in the memories of those who knew him or her. Still other people say they don't know what happens after death. You may already have your own ideas about what happens after death. The question has no easy answers. You may find that over time you will come up with your own ideas.

Chapter 6

Accepting Your Parent's Death

Robin's Diary

More than a year has passed since she died. But I still cry every time I think about my mother. I feel so alone and sad. My life feels so empty without her. She was my best friend. I knew I could depend on her. I miss her more now than ever before. I dream about her a lot. Late at night I sometimes think I can hear her walking around the house.

Robin is finding it hard to accept the death of her mother. This happens a lot to both boys and girls. Sometimes it takes many years before you can accept that your mom or dad is really dead. That's true even for grown ups. It takes so long because you are trying to hold on to what you lost. What you lost was very important to you.

Kids who lose their parents have to give themselves time to accept their loss. It won't happen quickly. There will be times when the sadness leaves, only to return a day or two later. Don't get angry with yourself. There is no way to speed up what you are going through. Feelings as powerful as grief are not something that you can turn off, like a light switch.

The best thing you can do to help yourself is to talk about how you feel. Turn to a good friend. He or she will be glad to listen. Some kids keep a diary of their feelings. Others paint or draw. Some take up jogging or weight lifting. They are all trying to express their feelings. You may have your own ideas. Do whatever makes you feel better.

Why is it so hard for kids to accept death? When you're a kid, you're full of life. Everything is ahead of you. Everything around you is full of life. Perhaps you will go to college and become a doctor. Perhaps you will play professional basketball. Maybe you will be a movie star. It's all possible.

Your body is still growing. It's full of life. You're getting bigger and stronger. Death is the furthest thing from your mind. And it should be. And all this makes death seem impossible.

But death is a part of life. All living things die. That's true for plants, birds, dogs, cats, and people. No one likes to think about it. It's scary. Robin's

There are many ways to reach out and ask for help during times of extreme sadness. Friends, family, counselors, and hotlines are all just a phone call away.

father told her that even he gets frightened when the word is mentioned.

Robin said she understood that living things die. But why do some things die when they are young and still needed? No one really knows the answer to that.

Death doesn't mean that your parent can no longer be part of your life. Their influence can live on past their death. When Robin was about to start smoking, she asked herself a question. Would my mother be proud of me if I did this?

Robin is using her memory of her mother to help her make important decisions. Robin decided not to smoke. She knew it was something her mother would not have liked. Using memories of your lost parent to guide you is a way to keep their memory alive.

Peter's father died of cancer. Peter decided that he wanted to go to college and study biology. He hoped to help find a cure for cancer. He saw his plans as a way of honoring his father.

There are other ways that are just as good. Nancy's mother died of alcoholism. She decided to become a drug and alcohol counselor. She saw the results of her mother's drinking. Nancy wanted to teach children the dangers of alcohol. This is another way to honor a parent's memory.

For Abdul, the way to honor his father was a little different. He wasn't sure what he wanted to do after he graduated from high school. Perhaps

Doing things you enjoy can ease sadness after a personal tragedy.

he'd join the Army or work at the post office. But Abdul didn't want to wait that long to honor his father. Abdul volunteered to play with the younger children at the local orphanage. He believed his helping other children would please his father.

These are not the only ways to keep your parent's memory alive. There are many others. These kids were trying to make positive things come out of the deaths of their parents. This is hard. It is hard to get over your anger and your fear. It takes time and patience. But if you try, you will feel better.

Good friends share your life with you during good times as well as bad.

Chapter 7

What Friends Can Do to Help

Judy's Diary

I didn't know what to say. Joyce was on the telephone. She told me that her father just died. She sounded upset, like she was holding back tears. I didn't know what to do. I didn't want to say anything stupid. This has never happened to me before. The best I could come up with was "I'm sorry." That's not very much. I was afraid of putting my foot in my mouth and making things worse. I asked Joyce whether she wanted to take a walk and talk about it. She sounded happy about the offer.

Up to now, this book has been about what happens to a kid whose parent has died. But this chapter is about what you can do to help a friend who has lost a parent. Your support can be important. In some cases, your help can save a life.

Real friends want to help. But they often feel awkward. They aren't sure what to do or say. They are afraid that they will say something stupid and make matters worse. Friends that have already lost a parent are likely to be most understanding. But even those with both parents alive can help.

As a friend, the best thing you can do is listen. Make it easy for your friend to talk about the death of a parent. Go to a place where it's quiet. Avoid noisy places, like malls and school yards. Peaceful places, such as a park or basement, are good choices.

Listening doesn't mean having the right words to say. There are no right words. It does mean letting your friend do the talking. Don't force your friend to talk about a parent's death. But tell him or her that if he or she wants to talk about it, you will listen. Not everyone grieves in the same way.

Mary Ann may need to cry. She may get angry. Don't take it personally. She has suffered a great loss. You can also expect her to say things that don't make sense. But don't correct her. She is grieving. Remember, grieving is the feeling of sadness suffered when something special is gone.

Jonathan may tell you that he feels like a stranger in his own house. There's so much activity that there is no place for him to be left alone. His parent's friends are busy making funeral arrangements and cooking food. But no one has taken a moment to talk with him. Sometimes kids get pushed aside when tragedy strikes. Adults forget that kids grieve. They think that they are too young to feel sad or to understand death. But kids get sad, too.

There are times when a friend can save a life. Watch out for danger signals. If your friend says he or she wants to join her lost parent in heaven, immediately tell her living parent. Your friend may be threatening suicide (killing herself). Don't take it as a joke. Taking it seriously could save your friend's life.

A friend may try to get you to promise not to tell anyone how he feels. But this is a promise that you should not keep. Your friend is so upset that he may feel that his own life is worthless. Your friend is wrong. At dark moments, some people are overcome by grief. They can't see the value of their own lives. As a friend, you can tell someone how much he or she means to you. But that may not be enough. Don't ignore your friend's feelings. Tell someone. The best person to tell is the living parent. If for some reason that isn't possible, tell a pastor, priest, rabbi, or school official. Don't keep it to yourself.

Your best efforts to help may not be enough. Your friend may need to get help from adults whose job it is to help people in pain. (There is a list at the back of the book that tells where people can get help. Counselors receive special training at helping others grieve. They feel comfortable talking about death. They see it as a natural part of life. Many hospitals and hospices employ grief counselors. A grief counselor understands the stages of grief that a person goes through. Pastors, priests, and rabbis have also been trained at helping people grieve.

Remember, the best help you can give is to make your friends understand that they are not alone. Let them know that you care, and so do their other friends and family. At first your friends may not believe you. In time they will see that you are telling the truth. With your help, and with time, the pain will pass.

Glossary—*Explaining New Words*

coffin A wooden box in which the body is buried. Also called a casket.

cremate To change a body to ashes by burning. The ashes are often kept in an urn or a small jar.

defense Something you use to hold back a flood of feelings.

denial Blocking true feelings.

depression Feeling low; constantly sad.

eulogy A speech given at a funeral.

foster care Temporary care of children by people who are not the real parents.

funeral A memorial service before the burial of someone who has died.

grief counselor A person trained to help others deal with their sorrow.

grieving Feeling sad.

hospice A place where dying people go to receive special care.

mausoleum A building where coffins are stored above ground.

mourning The way grief is shown.

suicide The act of killing yourself on purpose.

terminal disease Illness that ends in death.

urn Container that holds the ashes of a cremated person.

Where to Get Help

The Compassionate Friends can help if a family member has died. To find the support group nearest you, contact:

Compassionate Friends
P.O. Box 1347
Oakbrook, Illinois 60521
312-323-5010

Sometimes, when a parent dies, kids need to be with an adult of their same sex. Big Brothers of America helps a boy find a man to spend time with; Big Sisters is for girls.

Big Brothers or Big Sisters of America
220 Suburban Station Building
Philadelphia, Pennsylvania 19106

Make Today Count is for people dying of cancer. Get the address of the group nearest you from:

National Make Today Count Office
P.O Box 303
Burlington, Iowa 52601
319-753-6521

For Further Reading

Blume, Judy. *Tiger Eyes.* Scarsdale, NY: Bradbury Press, 1981. (Fiction) Davey Wexler's father is murdered. This story shows how his mother and brother cope with his death.

LeShan, Eda. *Learning to Say Goodby: When a Parent Dies.* New York: Avon Book, 1988. This book shows the way that a real family handled the death of a parent.

Krementz, Jill. *How It Feels When a Parent Dies.* New York: Alfred A. Knopf, 1981. The author spoke with nearly 20 kids about how they reacted and dealt with the death of a parent.

Rabb, Robert A. *Coping with Death.* New York: Rosen Publishing Group, 1989. This book talks about death and the place it has in life.

Rofes, Eric and the Unit at Fayerweather Street School. *The Kids' Book About Death and Dying.* Boston: Little Brown and Company,

1985. Written by 14 kids and their teacher, this book is about how and why death happens.

Spies, Karen Bornemann. *Everything You Need To Know About Grieving.* New York: Rosen Publishing Group, 1990. The author covers the many ways people deal with the sadness that comes with the loss of someone special.

Index

About the Author

Fred Bratman is a freelance writer and editor whose work has appeared in leading national magazines. Recently, he authored a book for teenagers entitled, "War in the Persian Gulf." He lives in New York City with his wife, Robin.

Acknowledgments and Photo Credits

Cover photo by Chuck Peterson.
Photograph on page 29: Chris Volpe. All other photographs by Stuart Rabinowitz.

Design/Production: Blackbirch Graphics, Inc.